First published in the United States
of America in 1990 by The Mallard Press

Mallard Press and its accompanying design
and logo are trademarks of BDD Promotional
Book Company, Inc.

Produced by
Twin Books
15 Sherwood Place
Greenwich, CT 06830

ISBN 0 792 45402 2

Printed in Hong Kong

DISNEY'S
MICKEY MOUSE
IN
THE BARRACUDA TRIANGLE

Written by
Floyd Norman

TWIN BOOKS

MALLARD PRESS

6

Another submarine carrying top-secret laser missiles had disappeared while cruising the high seas. The vessel had sent a radio call for help, but the message had been cut off. The government was even more baffled when yet another sub vanished a few days later. All the submarines and their crews had disappeared from the same location—a mysterious body of water known as the Barracuda Triangle.

At a secret navy base, Admiral Beagle was looking at a map marked with the last known locations of the missing subs. He knew that he needed a special agent to handle this assignment, someone with courage, resourcefulness and a spirit of adventure. The obvious choice was Mickey Mouse.

Late that night Mickey found himself in a long black limousine speeding toward the base. The assignment sounded dangerous, but Mickey could never resist an adventure.

If it was adventure Mickey was looking for, he was about to get it. Admiral Beagle told him that he would be aboard the next laser-missile sub to enter the Barracuda Triangle. This sub would carry the latest electronic detection equipment, as well as a miniature one-man sub that could be used as an escape vehicle.

The next morning, as they set sail for the dreaded Barracuda Triangle, Mickey and the ship's commander talked about the mission.

"Relax, Mickey," smiled the Commander. "Those new laser missiles we carry can defend us against anything."

"They didn't help the other ships," Mickey pointed out.

"But we're forewarned," answered the commander, "and we can depend on our special electronic detection equipment."

The sub reached the Barracuda Triangle and began its dive. Suddenly, the lights in the control room began to flicker. All the detection equipment stopped working, and the sub was dead in the water.

"We're under attack!" shouted the commander. "Fire the laser missiles!"

Not one missile would fire. When Mickey looked through the periscope, he could hardly believe his eyes. Rising from the water in front of them was what looked like a wall of steel. Suddenly, the wall parted, and the helpless submarine was sucked toward it. Mickey ran for the mini-sub. He had to escape. It was the only hope for the crew of the doomed submarine.

Mickey's tiny vessel was small and fast enough to get away from the force that was pulling the sub into its mysterious depths. As he sped away, Mickey saw that the "steel monster" was really a huge, sub-swallowing tanker ship!

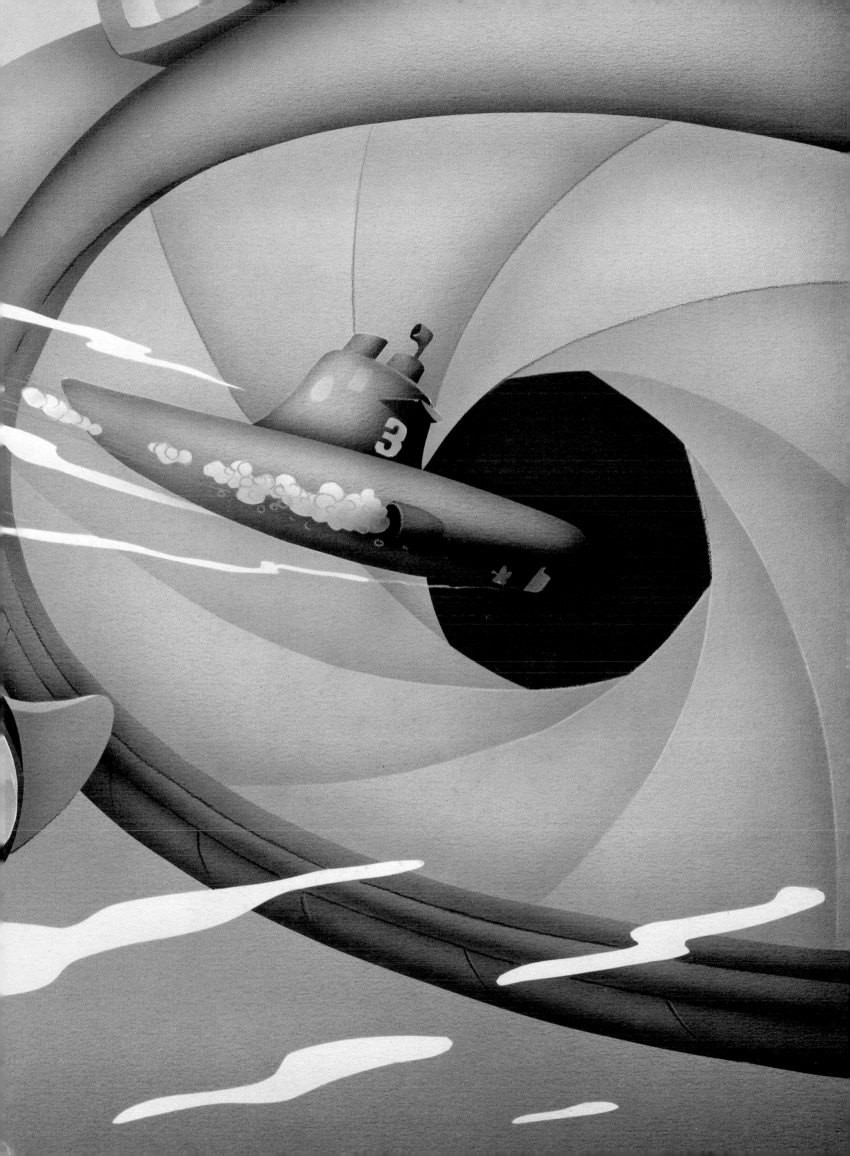

Mickey surfaced and circled the huge vessel, trying to find a weak spot. Suddenly, the ship began to shimmer. Mickey rubbed his eyes, but when he looked again, the huge ship had simply vanished. Nothing remained but a calm sea and a few curious sea gulls.

Mickey was alone in a tiny sub in the middle of the Barracuda Triangle. The submarine and its crew had been hijacked. Worse, the thing that had done the awful deed was nowhere to be found.

Mickey began to search. Maybe he could find some trace or clue. He was moving ahead cautiously when the sub suddenly stopped with a loud *clang!* He had hit something.

Mickey climbed out of the submarine and felt around under the water in front of the mini-sub. There was something there, all right—something he couldn't see.

Suddenly, mysterious forms were bobbing in the waves all around him. He was surrounded by dark-suited scuba divers, all carrying harpoon guns!

"What a pleasant surprise," one of them said. "Our special guest has finally arrived!"

Under armed guard, Mickey was marched to the bridge of the huge ship.

"Welcome, Mickey Mouse," grinned the evil commander. "I am Admiral Vulture. I want to thank you for bringing me the last thing I need for this operation— another hundred laser missiles. My master plan can now proceed."

As they steamed toward the center of the Triangle, Admiral Vulture bragged to Mickey about how he had captured the submarines by equipping his huge ship with a stealth device that made it invisible. He needed the stolen subs' laser missiles. "Now that I have enough of those weapons, I can rule the world!" he said triumphantly.

Admiral Vulture sat Mickey down in front of his command console. "You have played an important role in this historic event, Mr. Mouse," said the evil Admiral, "so it is only right that you should be rewarded. The very missiles you brought shall be the ones to force your country to its knees!"

"You'll never get away with this!" shouted Mickey, leaping up and grabbing for the Admiral's gun.

The Admiral's henchmen caught Mickey before he could reach their leader.

"I see you can't watch quietly, Mr. Mouse," said the Admiral. "Tie him to that table," he ordered. Hanging next to the table was a strange-looking device.

The Admiral flipped a switch and the device began to glow. "I wouldn't move if I were you, Mr. Mouse," laughed Vulture. "That is only a small laser, but it can cut through the hardest metal. I don't think it would have any difficulty with you."

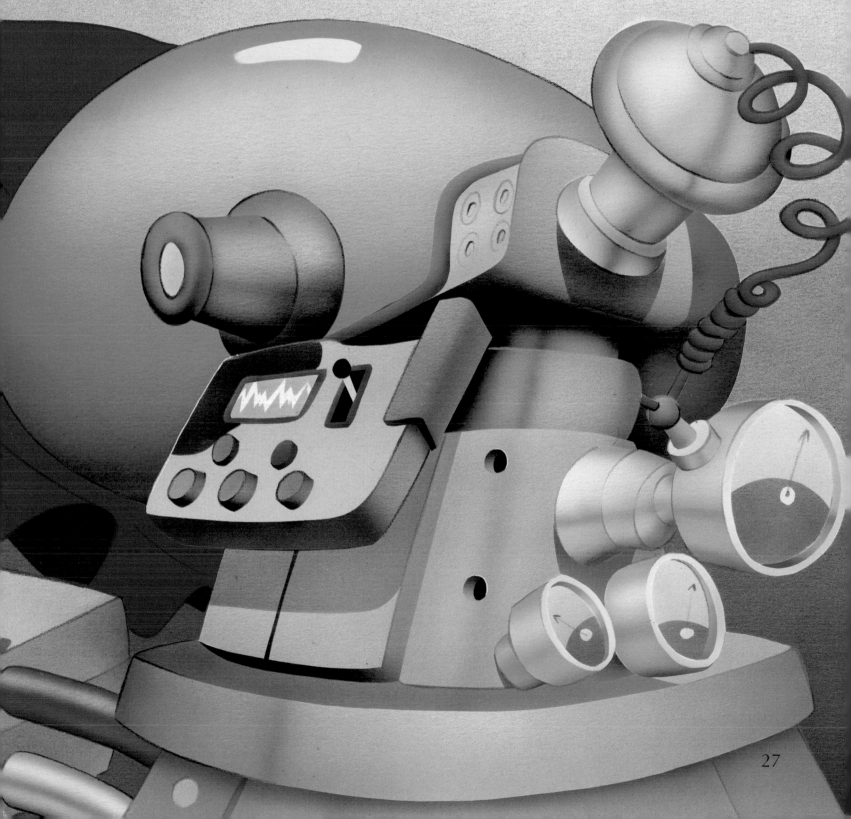

"W-why are you doing this?" stammered Mickey.
"Because I'm the bad guy," laughed the Admiral.
Mickey began to struggle against his bonds.
"Very well, Mr. Mouse," Vulture said, reaching over to turn the model laser on Mickey. "I guess you won't get to witness my triumph."
But before Vulture could aim the laser at him, Mickey strained forward and gave it a hard kick.

The laser beam spun crazily around the room, making everyone dive for cover.

"Look out," the evil Admiral shouted, "or we'll be sliced up like a stack of cold cuts!"

The white-hot beam cut a hole in the floor. The table Mickey was strapped to fell through the hole and landed with a crash on the level below.

The table crashed to pieces, and Mickey was free. He
ran down a long corridor, looking for a way out.
Suddenly, he heard voices.

"Over here! Help us!"

Mickey turned a corner and found the crews from the
captured submarines. The Admiral had kept them all
locked up in his huge ship. Mickey looked for a way to
free them, but a special power control kept the doors
shut tight. It looked as if the only way to free them was
to stop Admiral Vulture.

Mickey had an idea. "I've got to get to our sub!" he told himself.
Mickey found the hold where Admiral Vulture had stored the stolen
submarines and ran into the missile room of the one he had been aboard.
After a few minutes of frantic work, he made his way back to Admiral
Vulture's command center. The guards immediately captured him.

"Your feeble attempts to escape have failed, Mr. Mouse. Now you must
watch me make my first move toward ruling the world."

Admiral Vulture pressed a button, launching the first laser beam.
"Watch the birdie, Mr. Mouse," he cackled.

"*Your* missile is headed for *your* country, Mr. Mouse," the Admiral said slyly. "It will be the first to bow to me as world leader."

"You'd better check your screen again, Admiral Vulture," said Mickey. "That missile is headed right for this ship."

Admiral Vulture looked back to the monitor screen. The direction of the rocket's flight *had* changed!

The rocket was making a turn that pointed it back toward the ship.

"Fools!" the Admiral shouted at his henchmen. "What have you done? We'll all be blown to smithereens when that missile strikes!"

Admiral Vulture's henchmen began scrambling like rats. Some of them ran for the lifeboats and some just jumped overboard—anything to get away from that incoming laser missile.

Mickey tried to pull away, but the Admiral held him fast.

"You won't escape me, Mickey Mouse," he growled. "When this ship is vaporized, we'll both go with it."

The rocket zoomed out of the sky and landed on the ship with a dull thud.

"W-what?" gasped Admiral Vulture. "It didn't explode!"

"That's right," smiled Mickey. "Before you caught me again, I disarmed all the missiles on board our sub—the ones you were going to use first. They were duds, just like your plan to rule the world."

Mickey pressed a button that freed the submarine crews. They soon had their fleeing captors locked up.

Mickey sailed the huge ship containing the top-secret submarines back to the base, where Admiral Beagle congratulated him on a job well done.

"Good work, Mickey," smiled Beagle. "That evil tanker has swallowed its last submarine."

"Right!" chuckled Mickey. "I guess you could say the Barracuda Triangle has lost its bite."